In the world of *Sweet Pickles,* each animal gets into a pickle because of an all too human personality trait.

This book is about Doubtful Dog. He doubts anything and everything, especially himself.

Books in the Sweet Pickles Series:

WHO STOLE ALLIGATOR'S SHOE?
SCAREDY BEAR
FIXED BY CAMEL
NO KICKS FOR DOG
ELEPHANT EATS THE PROFITS
FISH AND FLIPS
GOOSE GOOFS OFF
HIPPO JOGS FOR HEALTH
ME TOO IGUANA
JACKAL WANTS MORE
WHO CAN TRUST YOU, KANGAROO?
LION IS DOWN IN THE DUMPS
MOODY MOOSE BUTTONS
NUTS TO NIGHTINGALE
OCTOPUS PROTESTS
PIG THINKS PINK
QUAIL CAN'T DECIDE
REST RABBIT REST
STORK SPILLS THE BEANS
TURTLE THROWS A TANTRUM
HAPPY BIRTHDAY UNICORN
KISS ME, I'M VULTURE
VERY WORRIED WALRUS
XERUS WON'T ALLOW IT!
YAKETY YAK YAK YAK
ZIP GOES ZEBRA

Library of Congress Cataloging in Publication Data

Hefter, Richard.
No kicks for Dog.

(Sweet Pickles series)
SUMMARY : Dog's self-esteem is so low that he doubts he can do anything well.
[1. Dogs—Fiction] I. Title. II. Series:

PZ7.H3587Nm [E] 78-17009
ISBN 0-03-042011-3

Published simultaneously in Canada by Holt, Rinehart and Winston of Canada, Limited.

Printed in the United States of America
Weekly Reader Books' Edition

Weekly Reader Books presents

NO KICKS FOR DOG

Written and illustrated by Richard Hefter
Edited by Ruth Lerner Perle

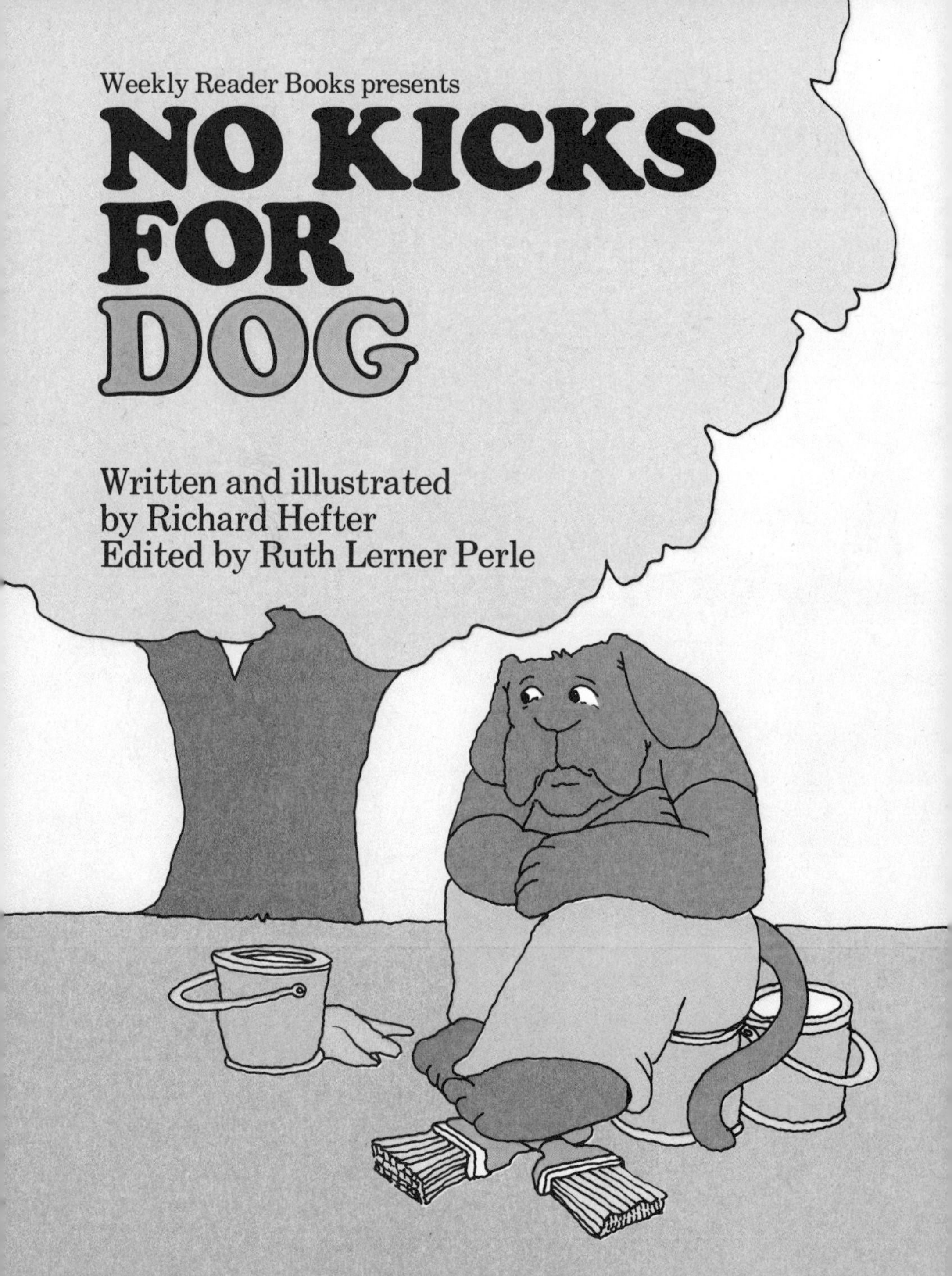

Holt, Rinehart and Winston • New York

Yak and Hippo were jogging through the park. They saw Dog sitting on a bench, surrounded by pails and brushes and rags.

“Good morning, Dog,” huffed Hippo. “Would you like to come along with us? We are going to play ball.”

“I don’t think so,” sighed Dog. “I’m not very good at games. Besides, I have an awful lot to do right now and I don’t think I can.”

"Nonsense," laughed Yak. "Anybody can! It's just a simple matter of throwing and catching and kicking and..."

“I didn’t mean *that*,” said Dog. “I meant that I don’t think I can do the work I promised to do today. I told Jackal I would paint his fence and I don’t know how.”

"Nonsense," giggled Yak. "Anybody can paint a fence. Why, painting a fence is as easy as falling off a log."

"I doubt it," moaned Dog. "It seems like a very difficult thing to me. I don't know anything about painting fences, and I'm not very good at doing things I don't know about."

"Don't worry, Dog," puffed Hippo. "We will show you how to do it. Just follow us and everything will be all right."

"I doubt it," mumbled Dog.

They picked up the pails and paints and rags and brushes and walked over to Jackal's house. On the way, they met Walrus.

"Good morning," said Walrus. "You'd better be careful with all those pails and things. You could slip and hurt yourselves."

"Don't worry," smiled Yak. "We're old hands at this painting business. Everything is under control."

"I doubt it," said Dog.

Walrus followed them down the street. They ran into Pig.

"Hi there," smiled Pig. "Where are you all going?"

"We're going to show Dog how to paint a fence," said Yak. "He said he didn't think he knew how to do it and Hippo and I told him we would give him instructions and Walrus came along too and everything is under control now that we are all here."

"I doubt it," grumbled Dog.

Pig joined them.
They marched over to the fence around Jackal's house.

"Here we are," said Yak. "Now we can get started. The first thing to do is to get all these cans of paint open."

"Oh, no!" cried Walrus. "First you have to spread out the rags so they catch all the drips."

“The brushes,” puffed Hippo. “First get the brushes.”

“The pails,” cried Pig. “You pour the paint in the pails first.”

“Don’t worry, Dog,” shouted Yak. “Everything is under control. You’ll see how easy it is to paint a fence.”

“I doubt it,” moaned Dog.

Yak started to open all the cans of paint.
Walrus started spreading out the rags and bumped into Hippo.
Hippo dropped the brushes and fell against Pig.
Pig fell and tossed the buckets up into the air.

"LOOK OUT!" screeched Yak as a bucket landed on his head with a plop.

SPLOSH. Yak dropped the paint.

"Get out of my way!" yelled Hippo as he slipped on the wet paint.

"You see!" shouted Yak from inside the bucket. "There's nothing to it if you start in an organized way. Anyone can paint a fence, even you!"

"I doubt it," groaned Dog.

"Have no fear," smiled Hippo. "You just start painting right here at the top and before you know it the whole fence will be finished."

Hippo started painting.

"No, no!" screamed Yak. "You start from the bottom and use sideways strokes like this!"

Yak started painting.

"That's not right," moaned Walrus. "You should always start carefully in the middle like this."

Walrus started painting.

"Excuse me guys," smiled Pig. "I'm positive Dog wants to learn the proper way to paint a fence. And that means you start on the end with up and down strokes."

Pig started painting.

Hippo bumped into Yak.
Yak backed into Walrus.
Walrus fell on top of Pig.
"OUCH!" wailed Walrus. "Someone poked me with a brush."
"HELP!" screeched Yak. "I'm getting full of paint!"

They all bumped and scuffled and fell against the fence with a bang.

"Somebody kicked me!" cried Hippo.

"Get your foot out of my face," yelled Pig. "Please."

They dripped and sploshed and sloshed paint all over the fence.

Dog watched.

Finally, Yak turned around and said to Dog, "*Now* you see how simple it is to paint the fence, right?"

"Wrong," grumped Dog.

“But,” cried Pig, “surely you know how to paint the fence now.”

“Nope,” said Dog.

“Come on, Dog! You can get a kick out of painting the fence,” added Hippo.

“No kicks for me,” said Dog.

“But Dog,” wailed Walrus. “I know you can paint the fence.”

“I doubt it,” mumbled Dog.

"WHY CAN'T YOU PAINT THE FENCE, DOG?" shouted Yak and Pig and Hippo and Walrus.

"Because it's already painted," said Dog, and he walked away kicking a can in front of him.

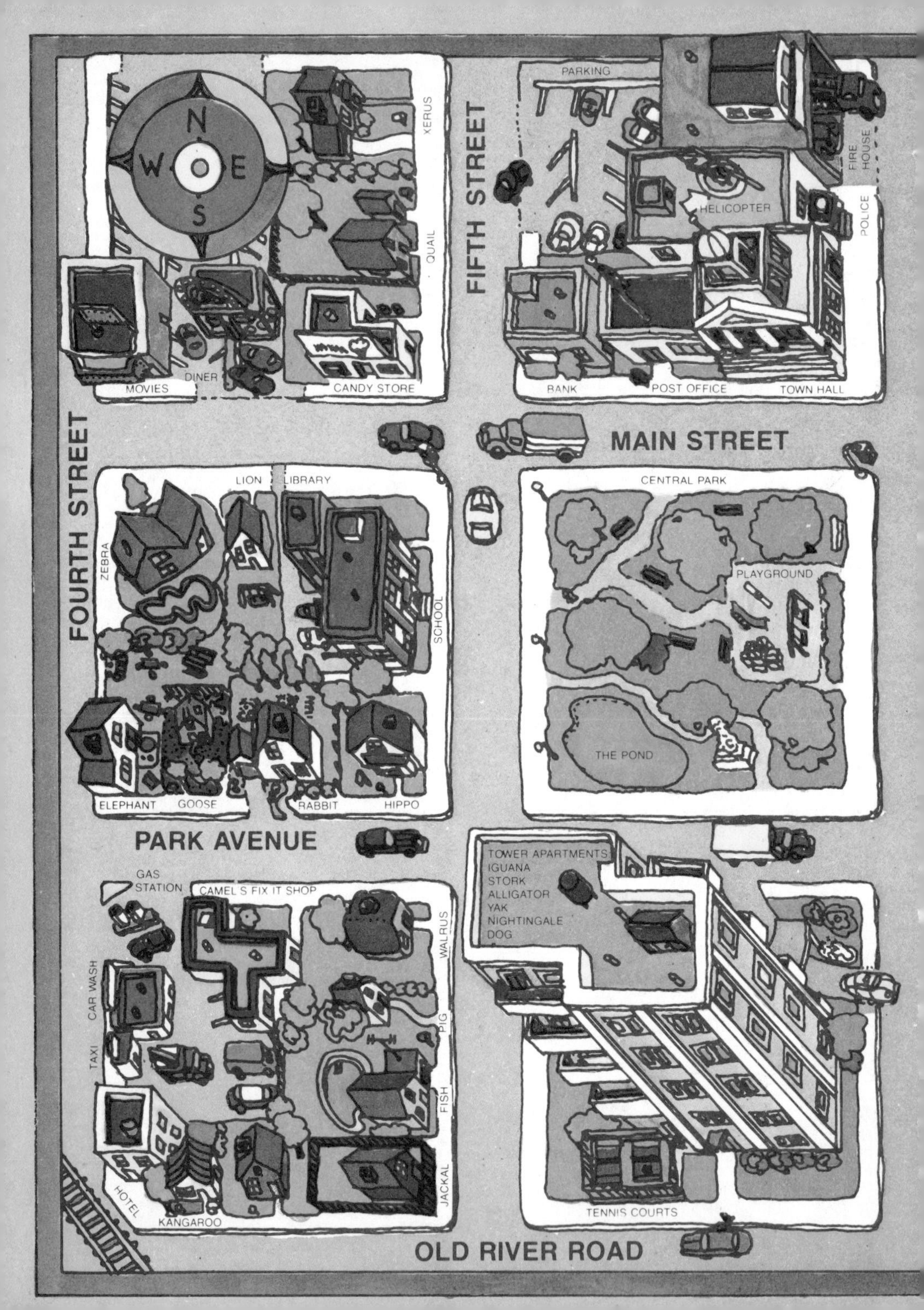
N
W
E
S
PARKING
FIFTH STREET
XERUS
QUAIL
FIRE HOUSE
POLICE
HELICOPTER
MOVIES
DINER
CANDY STORE
BANK
POST OFFICE
TOWN HALL
MAIN STREET
FOURTH STREET
LION
LIBRARY
ZEBRA
SCHOOL
CENTRAL PARK
PLAYGROUND
THE POND
ELEPHANT
GOOSE
RABBIT
HIPPO
PARK AVENUE
GAS STATION
CAMEL'S FIX IT SHOP
WALRUS
TOWER APARTMENTS
IGUANA
STORK
ALLIGATOR
YAK
NIGHTINGALE
DOG
CAR WASH
TAXI
PIG
FISH
JACKAL
HOTEL
KANGAROO
TENNIS COURTS
OLD RIVER ROAD